THE ISLAND SAMPLER

LEAH R CUTTER

Knotted Road Press

Come someplace new…
Are you a traveler? Do you enjoy exploring strange new worlds, new cultures, new people?

Journey into the various lands envisioned by Leah Cutter.

Sign up for my newsletter and I'll start you on your travels with a free copy of my book, *The Island Sampler*.

I will never spam you or use your email for nefarious purposes. You can also unsubscribe at any time.

http://www.LeahCutter.com/newsletter/

CONTENTS

HISTORIC/EPIC FANTASY

INTRODUCTION

Welcome to the Island Sampler!

Why do I call this the Island Sampler?

Like many writers, I write all over the map.

I primarily write fantasy, but I write many different flavors of fantasy. I'm best known for my historic fantasy ("Paper Mage", the first book I sold to a New York publisher).

But I also write fantasy with shapeshifters (the Shadow Wars trilogy, that starts with "The Raven and the Dancing Tiger.") As well as more rural fantasy with clockwork fairies. And changelings.

And I write mysteries—I've had more than one short story published in "Alfred Hitchcock's Mystery Magazine." I also write science fiction stories. And post-apocalyptic fairy tales. And…

You get the point.

The problem with writing so many differently flavors of fantasy under a single name is that it makes it difficult for readers to find what they like. In the old days, my publisher would make me have a different pen name for every genre. But that was yesterday. As I am now indie publishing all of these titles, I am responsible for figuring out the marketing.

It's fairly easy to distinguish the science fiction from the fantasy.

But how do I categorize the different types of fantasy? Particularly when so much of what I write falls under the category of "contemporary fantasy" and yet it's all so different?

For example, I write what I call "immersive fiction." It isn't slow paced, almost everything I write is page-turning fiction. However, in these books, I draw the readers very deep into the world, immerse them in the everydayness of the place.

At the opposite end of the spectrum, I write really high-energy fiction, where, "OMG the world is going to end in seventeen minutes!"

A reader who thoroughly enjoys the immersive fiction may or may not enjoy the high-energy, high-stakes fiction, and vice versa. I have readers who tell me that my immersive fiction books are their favorites and they don't like the other things I write. I've had readers absolutely love the world-about-to-end fiction, who found the immersive fiction boring.

So how do I guide readers? How do I help them find the types of books that they like to read?

Since I write all over the map, I came up with the concept of actually creating a map. For me, the axis of the map turned out to be:

—Up and down (Y), I put the far future at the top and the past at the bottom.

—Across the bottom (X), I grade books from low energy to high energy.

Once I figured out my axis, I placed all my titles on it, figuring out where each one landed.

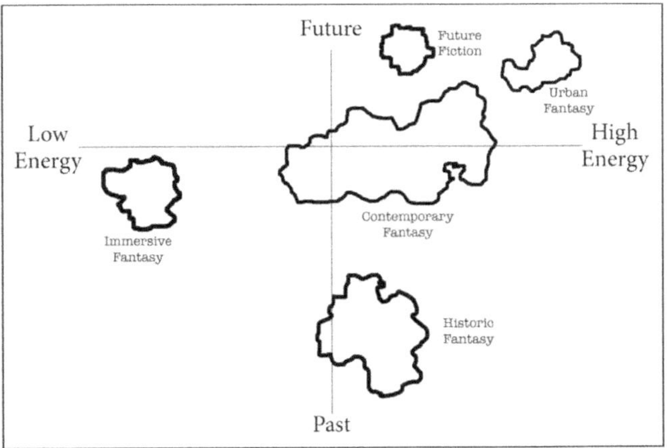

This helped me to see that I have five separate islands of fiction. Hence, the Island Sampler.

I've tried to give you the "flavor" of each island, either by including the first chapter of one of the novels that I would put in that part of the map, or with a short story.

Don't be surprised if the spices from one island delights you, while the spices from a different island aren't to your taste. This is a sampler, so you get to try all of the different flavors in package and find the island that suits you best.

Enjoy!

CONTEMPORARY FANTASY

IF YOU LOOK AT THE MAP, YOU'LL SEE THAT THE ISLAND OF contemporary fantasy is the largest, by far. This appears to be where my heart is. Though I love writing other things, my pen keeps finding its way back here.

I often think about my contemporary fantasy as "fairies in the backyard". Rarely do I write about overt magic or worlds that are known for being magical. Instead, the magic is always hidden, part of a secret world that only a few stumble into.

Frequently I write about shapeshifters, though not like werewolves. More like *kitsune* who have a fox form, or raven, or even trolls. And yes, I frequently have a lot of Asian influence in my stories.

CONTEMPORARY FANTASY NOVELS

The Seattle Trolls Trilogy
The Changeling Troll
The Princess Troll
The Fairy Bridge Troll

The Shadow Wars Trilogy
The Raven and the Dancing Tiger
The Guardian Hound
War Among the Crocodiles

The Clockwork Fairy Kingdom
The Clockwork Fairy Kingdom
The Maker, the Teacher, and the Monster
The Dwarven Wars

Other
Zydeco Queen and the Creole Fairy Courts

CONTEMPORARY FANTASY SAMPLE

URBAN FANTASY

I don't have a lot of novels that are truly urban fantasy. The current definition for the genre includes:

- A kickass chick with powers
- Supernatural beings
- The city as a character

Most of the time, you'll see urban fantasy novels with a young woman who has a bare midriff, holding a sword or a gun or some other weapon. The colors are super saturated. The city behind her looks ominous.

I've taken a little different approach. My main characters tend to be sarcastic. Cassie, in particular, has a foul mouth (uses the word "Fuck" like a comma) and is likely to laugh at your pitiful attempt to take over the world.

URBAN FANTASY SAMPLE

THIS SHORT STORY IS ACTUALLY THE BASIS FOR A SERIES OF stories about *Huli* Transport. It was originally published in *Fiction River: Hex in the City*.

FOX AND HOUND

"You need bicycle taxi? Rickshaw?" Gou asked for the ten-thousandth time, trying to catch the eye of yet another tourist pouring off the late afternoon train from Hong Kong. He wore his second best shirt, the one with the fake American brand logo on the front pocket, that made him look more official, as well as his lightest-weight beige slacks, and rubber sandals. It was far too hot to wear jeans, though he had two pairs that he kept pristine and folded up at the noodle shop his mom ran.

Gou wasn't supposed to be in the West Beijing station, of course. The guards weren't supposed to let anyone without a ticket or a license into the huge concrete courtyard in the front of the massive station, let alone into the echoing, noisy halls close to the trains.

But Gou paid Shu well, and often, which got him into the station next to the staircase coming up from the trains, where he could get tourists to follow him before they headed to the subway stop. Stretching away from the bottom of the stairs and off into the distance were *li* upon *li* of railway lines going to places Gou had no hope of seeing. Loud speakers with polite, nasal accents announced the times and train numbers to places Gou had only heard in stories told by his grandmother.

Only a few other bicycle taxies drivers were still waiting at the top of the stairs, mainly old men who needed a fare as badly as Gou, but who didn't speak enough English or wanted to work hard enough. Gou's friends were already gone: Hy with his official green uniform and colorful, laminated maps had snagged an entire group, while Long Yen with his charm and smile had persuaded an American couple to follow him.

"Best ride in town," Gou assured a western woman with strange blue eyes and brown curls poking around the sides of a wide brimmed hat. "Very smooth, very cheap." She shook her head and pulled the straps of her huge pack tighter, as if she was afraid Gou would rip it off her back.

Gou rolled his eyes and turned back to the few stragglers. He had to get a fare this afternoon. He needed the money. The platform in the back of his bicycle taxi, where his passengers put their feet, had broken off. He'd needed to buy a new one, and he'd had to pay to get it attached: The welder wouldn't barter trips with him.

Shu would be there tomorrow, demanding his cut. And Gou couldn't be short, or he'd lose his access to the train station. He might even be forced to join Hy, and work for a real company, where he'd never make enough money for his dreams. As an independent, if he hustled enough, at least he stood a chance.

Only a couple of straggling tourists remained, and they wouldn't even look at Gou, these tall white people with their big packs that they carried on both their front and back, as if they were taking all their possessions as well as their children with them.

The other drivers left, but Gou hung on, just for a bit, hoping.

Maybe he could work the northern night market tonight, hauling either drunken tourists or merchants and their goods. But the last time he'd done that, he'd ended up working for a fisherman and his cart had *stank* for a week.

However, he had to get the money somehow.

Gou turned to go and almost walked into an Asian man standing right beside him. *"Duibuqi,"* he said, automatically apologizing.

The man replied in English. "You have a taxi?"

"Bicycle rickshaw," Gou said with his best customer smile. "Faster than cars and traffic," he assured the man.

His potential customer wore a crisp, white, short-sleeved shirt, brand new jeans, and Western sandals. He had a sharp nose and chin, like they'd been pinched out of clay. Freckles scattered across his nose, and his hair had been cut short, possibly too short, as it highlighted oversized ears and a broad forehead.

Beside the man, a large black trunk stood, almost waist high, with gold molding on the corners and around the lock.

"Best service in Beijing," Gou assured the man, reaching for the leather handle on the top of the trunk and tugging.

It didn't budge.

The man smiled at Gou. "Can you take me to *Huli Hutong*?"

"Of course," Gou boasted, though he had no idea where that was. If the man had actually pronounced the Mandarin correctly, it would have translated into Fox Lane. It didn't matter, though. Gou could find anything in this city.

The man laughed. "Very well, then," he said.

Just like that, the trunk came off the floor. It was heavy, and it didn't have wheels like most foreign luggage. However, Gou was strong, and he worked to make it look easy to carry. He led the way across the expansive, brown-marble entranceway, weaving around the huge pillars, and out into the soft night air.

The concrete courtyard was still full of people. Gou had heard more than one American tourist compare it to a football field. He glanced behind him, but his fare wasn't staring with wide-eyed amazement. He'd either been in China for a while, or he'd been here before.

Gou nodded to the boy who watched all the bikes, to make sure they didn't get stolen, past the other peddle cabs where the owners were stretched out, reading or napping, all the way to his own little brown and yellow cab.

His cab wasn't licensed, but Gou had spray painted numbers on the back of it, to make it look official. The brown seats were filled with rubber he'd scavenged from the side of the road, that his sister had sewn together. They smelled funny sometimes when it was too hot, but they were more comfortable than most of the other seats Gou had tried. The yellow cover that unfurled over the seats was patched, yet it was still mostly water proof. Gou kept the wheel bearings and the frame oiled and rust free, and the brakes tight.

"You from out of town?" Gou asked as he hoisted the trunk onto one side of the carriage.

"Yes, I'm visiting here from Japan," the man admitted.

Gou raised his eyebrows at that. China didn't have the greatest relationship with Japan, and Gou had met very few visitors from there. "Ah, *konichiwa,*" Gou said, bowing his head.

The man replied with a flurry of Japanese.

Gou held up his hands and shook his head. "I only know a few words," he said. According to his mother, his father had been Japanese, or had come from there. But he hadn't stuck around, something Gou's step-father reminded him of at almost every dinner they ate together.

His mother had insisted that Gou learn a few words in the language, however, Gou hadn't stuck to it.

"Pity," the man said, peering closely at Gou. "I would have thought—never mind. You speak good English, though," he said, settling into his seat.

"Thank you," Gou said, climbing onto his bike. "I practice. But

I need more." More work. More money. More time. More powerful relations who could smooth his way.

The man laughed. "We all need more," he said softly.

GOU BUMPED HIS WAY ACROSS THE CRACKED CONCRETE, UP across the sidewalk, and into the bike lane along Fuxing Lu. He automatically started peddling east, going toward the heart of Beijing. It was late enough in the day that many workers rode around him on their black, sturdy bikes. Every time one passed Gou, they rang their bell. Cars filled the road, bumper-to-bumper. Pollution hazed the air across the eight lanes of traffic, and stank of rotten eggs, wood smoke, and burnt oil. Gou had worn his mask when he peddled into the station, but he couldn't put it on now: He didn't want to scare the tourist, and maybe not get a good tip.

"First time in Beijing?" Gou called out over his shoulder.

"No, no. I have family here," the man assured him.

When Gou stopped at Wanfeng Lu, he realized he didn't know where he was going. "*Huli Hutong*?" he called back as he stood on his peddles to get his bicycle moving again.

"Yes," the man replied.

Gou didn't have to look back to know he was being laughed at.

"It's near *Dai Tong*," the man called out helpfully.

Gou peddled and thought, rolling out a map of Beijing in his mind. *Dai Tong* neighborhood was south of the city, and not too far from the railroad station, just the next big circle in. It wasn't a tourist place, so he hadn't gone there often. But maybe...

"Is it near *Ji lu*?" Gou asked, remembering a small neighborhood near the east corner of *Dai Tong*—Chicken Street, close to a night market that specialized in many chicken dishes, from feet to butts to tongues.

Plus, wouldn't the foxes want be close to the chickens?

"Very good!" the man called out.

Pleased, Gou peddled faster. Though he didn't know exactly where he was going, at least he wouldn't be circling forever. Maybe he could get a fare from the market there, before heading back to the noodle house that his mom ran to sleep.

The light dimmed and night settled in as Gou turned off the main thoroughfare and onto the side streets. Few cars remained here, and they were happy to blast their horns at him, making him jump, or blinding him with their lights. But it was only a few more blocks before he could slip into the smaller hutong streets, where cars weren't allowed.

Gou didn't mind driving down a hutong during the day, but he hated it at night: Light came only from a few lanterns hanging outside of house gates, as well as from windows. No overhead lights lit the narrow alleyways. It was impossible to avoid the deep ruts in the road, or the broken stones. He winced every time he heard the board in the passenger cab groan. He didn't have the money to fix it again.

The smell of chicken and garlic, frying in a wok, floated out to Gou. He hadn't eaten dinner—and he was never sure if his mom would leave anything for him at the noodle house. He couldn't afford much, not even with this fare, not with Shu's bribe due.

Beyond the tall walls that lined the tiny street, Gou heard the occasional radio or TV. They passed a doorway where half a dozen old men sat out on small chairs on the stoop, drinking shots. Two girls in navy blue, school uniforms walked slowly down the lane, only stepping to the side when Gou rang his bell.

"Turn here!" the man suddenly called out.

Gou turned immediately. An open gate sprang up before him, with a peaked roof and plain walls. He barely missed the edges, but managed to drive his cab directly through the center.

Hushed air fell on Gou, making him slow down. The street here was even more narrow here, and the old stone houses were only a few feet apart. Trees grew next to the walls, shading the street. Broken flagstones marred the path.

"Then another right here," the man said, his quiet voice echoing in the small space.

Gou pulled out of the tight alley into a broader street. It was funny—he couldn't hear the traffic beyond the walls, not even the motorcycles. And the air smelled sweeter. It didn't burn his lungs like the badly polluted air of the city usually did.

There were no cars on this street, not even parked, even though it was wide enough to hold them. Tall, brick fences lined the street, with doors that still glowed brilliant red even in the dark. Old fashioned lanterns hung outside each. Large, graceful trees rose up to form an arch overhead. Sweet night jasmine bloomed in the gardens. Jye's tired legs suddenly felt refreshed, as though he could peddle for ten thousand *li*.

"Down at the end of the street," the man said.

Gou nodded as he pulled into the cul-de-sac. The gate at the end was larger than the ones he'd passed. It must lead to a *shiheyuan*, or traditional courtyard. He could only imagine what lay beyond the gate, the many buildings lining the center square, the garden of brilliant flowers that he could almost smell, the burbling fountain that would give him peace in the middle of the night.

Gou pulled himself out of his day dream and turned to say, "Here?"

But the man had already hopped off Gou's bike and was tugging the large trunk to the ground.

"Let me help," Gou said, about to slide off his bicycle.

"No, no. Stay there," the man insisted. "You must not get off your bike."

"Really?" Gou asked.

The man gave him a toothy smile, like a foreigner. "Trust me. You need to stay on it."

Gou thought it was strange, but he did as he was told.

"How much do I owe you?" the man asked, getting out his wallet.

Gou quoted four times his usual price, expecting the man to bargain.

The man didn't even blink. He just counted out the *yuan* from a thick wad.

Gou could have kicked himself. He should have asked for more. The man could obviously afford it.

At least now he'd be able to pay Shu.

"Go straight back out the way we came in," the man instructed. "And don't get off your bike. You shouldn't have any trouble."

"Thank you," Gou said, carefully folding the bills, then shoving them into his front pocket. "*Xie xie nin.*"

"You're welcome," the man replied, waving it off and turning toward the gate.

Gou waited, hoping to catch a glimpse of what was inside the gate, but the man slipped through more quickly than Gou would have imagined, especially given that large trunk.

He sighed, then shook his head. Nothing more to do here but head back. He didn't need to get another fare, but maybe he could stop by the night market anyway, just in case his luck was still running hot.

Then Gou's stomach rumbled, reminding him that he hadn't eaten dinner yet.

Gou rode alone the open street, still marveling at how quiet and peaceful it all seemed. He nearly missed the alley, but luckily he was going slowly enough that he could bump into it.

Strange, though. Where had that temple come from? He hadn't seen it on the way in. He would have remembered the great rock *steeles* rising in front of it. Maybe he should stop and read what was carved into their sides—then his stomach rumbled again, and he passed by.

Then the gate he'd first come through rose in front of him. Good. He was going the right way.

Suddenly, from beside the gate, a great dog sprang out of nowhere. It looked like a Doberman, with great teeth and glowing red eyes. It leaped straight for Gou.

Gou kicked out with his foot, giving the dog a good hit in the face. The dog lunged again, but Gou kept going, peddling with one foot while kicking with the other.

He had to get out of there.

The dog charged one last time, banging into the back of Gou's rickshaw. He heard the metal groan, but he righted himself and peddled madly, popping through the gate.

Noise and light and the sour stench of pollution all returned suddenly. Gou stood on the brakes to slow down, then looked over his shoulder.

No dog from his nightmares bounded up after him.

And no gate stood behind him. It was just a blank wall. As if it had never been there.

Gou dismounted his bike, his legs shaking. If he'd fallen off, touched the ground in that cursed hutong, he would have been stuck there forever. He just knew it. It was like one of those fairy tales his grandmother had told him, though she'd always said the fox fairies were good.

But he'd escaped! Gou pumped his fist. What a story he had to tell his friends, later.

Then Gou stuck his hand in his pocket.

Instead of a nice folded square of *yuan*, he pulled out a crumpled pile of dead leaves.

Gou may have escaped, but he'd been cheated out of his money.

As soon as Gou finished working in his mom's noodle

shop the next morning, he peddled as fast as he could to *Dai Tong*, searching for the man who had cheated him. The day had dawned hot and smoggy, the radio announcing a smog index of one hundred eighteen, unhealthy for those sensitive to it. Gou wore his mask wrapped tightly across his face, as well as the same clothes he'd worn the day before.

The wall where the gate had been was still blank, made out of plain, gray brick. On the other side of the wall stood a house. Now, in the light of day, Gou could tell that this hutong wasn't one of those that had tours or tourists: The nearby walls slumped and were broken along the edges, the clay tiles on roofs were shattered, and laundry hung between the houses, like colorful flags. This was a place where people lived, not a park with tours. He could hear children playing just a few doors down, and the smells of thick *jitang* and spicy ginger floated to him.

The man was nowhere to be seen. Gou peddled through all the back lanes of *Dai Tong* before he raced to the train station, hoping to pick up at least one fare before Shu arrived and demanded his bribe.

The gods seemed to smile on Gou that morning, and he got double his normal fare from a Norwegian tourist with bad breath who was looking for, "Beer, beer, and more beer!" Gou was even able to pay Shu, counting out the *yuan* into his fat, sweating palm. Gou wouldn't have enough for a single repair, not even a flat tire, but the next fare should fix that.

Or finding the man who'd cheated him.

Every day, Gou spent his extra hours seeking the man, peddling through back alleys and tiny, twisted streets that no devil could follow. He even talked with some of the older peddle cab drivers, seeing if they had ever gone to either *Dai Tong* or heard of *Huli Hutong*, but none of them had.

It was early evening almost a month later when Gou finally found his prey. He was navigating *Yingtao San Hutong*, a very thin alley: If he'd had two passengers, each would have been able to touch a gray brick wall. The smog had thinned, and though the air index was above fifty, Gou wasn't wearing his mask. In the alcove next to him, neighbors had hung half a dozen birdcages, each holding a bright green or yellow songbird who sounded clear notes through the night.

Despite the cramped lane, a broom merchant had put out a big box out in front of his shop, with different types of brooms sticking out of it: Modern brooms made from bright blue and red plastic, western style brooms made of yellow straw, as well as traditional wooden brooms with brown branches tied to the end.

Gou slowed down even further, standing on the peddles while he waited for two high school girls in their uniforms to pass by first, admiring their white shirts and green plaid skirts. When he looked back up, he spied the man he was seeking coming out of the shop.

Without thinking, Gou slammed down on his peddles, flying forward and nearly running into the man.

The shop keeper came out from his doorway yelling, but Gou ignored him, focusing on the man carrying an odd shaped broom. "You cheated me," he said, getting off his bike.

"And you found me. Astonishing. You've been looking for a while, haven't you?" the man responded in perfect Mandarin.

"I have," Gou said, pulling up. The man had never spoken Mandarin before. He was Japanese, right?

"It's alright," the man said, both to the shopkeeper and to Gou. "This is my ride."

"Only if you pay me first. With real money," Gou said hotly. He wasn't about to be fooled again.

The man considered him. "Can you find your way to *Huli Hutong* by yourself?"

Gou bit his lip. He wanted to say that of course he could. But he hadn't been able to find it, not after all his weeks of searching.

"I will pay you double if you can get into the hutong alone," the man said, settling into the passenger cab of Gou's bike.

Gou refused to climb back onto his bike. "You pay me what you owe me. Now. In real money."

The man took out his wallet and carefully counted out the bills, like he had the first time. He waved them toward Gou, then took them back. "I could pay you this, now. And that would guarantee that you'd never see me again. No matter how hard you look. Ever. Or," the man continued slyly. "You could listen to a proposal."

"You haven't said anything of interest, yet," Gou said, scowling.

"I'm impressed that you found me, actually. You have potential, and I have a possible business deal," the man said calmly. "I want you, exclusively, to carry me and my family. You will need more bikes, motorbikes, even, and I will pay for them. You will own a whole fleet of cabs, that cater to us. But you have to be able to get to my home on your own. You've already proved that you can get out."

"You set that dog on me?" Gou asked hotly. He still had nightmares about those red eyes, though he told himself that it must have been a trick of the light.

The man shrugged. "You passed that test." He leaned forward. "Now pass this one." For a moment his eyes held a soft purple glow, then they faded back to plain black.

How could Gou find the unfindable? The street wasn't on any map, the hutong not in any history of the neighborhoods.

Still, Gou had to try, though Hy and Long Yen and everyone would call him a fool for not taking the money in hand and running.

With a sigh, he got back onto his bike, standing on the peddles to get the vehicle moving.

The man laughed in the clear evening air. "You have until midnight," he declared. "The hunt is on!"

Gou wasn't certain, though, if he was the fox or the hound.

It had grown dark by the time Gou reached *Dai Tong*, however, he was very familiar with the neighborhood now. He peddled directly to the place where he'd first seen the gate to *Huli Hutong*, though it was just a wall, as always. He rode next to the wall slowly, constantly looking up from where he was going to the plain brick, hoping to catch a glimpse of an opening, but he never saw one.

They passed dark doorways, closed shops, and barred windows, all the life tucked away behind the steep walls. Gou felt like the fences were closing in on him, the small alley growing more narrow. He didn't have a watch, or really, anything to tell time with: It was no longer ancient times, with bell towers ringing the double hours. Still, he knew it was late, and growing later.

Gou peddled faster, popping out of the lane and into a wider street. The cars there honked at him, flashing their lights, but he didn't care. He pulled in front of them, racing, his legs pumping, as he turned sharply, going back into the neighborhood, taking them down an even smaller alley.

If Gou leaned to the side, he could run his fingers along the wall here. He neatly avoided the flower box on his right, the sour smell of geraniums floating up to him, then the raft of bicycles all chained to a long metal pipe on his left. He still didn't see an entrance, though he slowed down and kept swiveling his head, looking from side to side.

They went down another alley, then another, always circling back to *Dai Tong*.

Finally, the man said, "Not everything can be seen."

Gou wanted to shout at his passenger. He knew that. He'd been looking and looking, and he'd never been able to find the entrance, find his way back into that quiet street.

As they reached the end of the alley, Gou paused. *Huli Hutong* hadn't just been beautiful to look at, it had also smelled wonderful, like sweet lilies. It had felt different too, the air softer, more humid. There hadn't been any traffic noises, it had been quiet. He was sure there were fountains that sang cheerfully behind the courtyard walls, and that the rice there would be fragrant and delicious.

Maybe Gou couldn't find it with his eyes. But with his ears, and his nose, and his mouth…

Gou erupted out into the wider street, urging his tired legs to go faster. He'd traveled far that day, but he was determined to go further yet. The car behind him honked angrily and swerved. Gou waved at him in apology, racing down the wide street, taking them back to the first alley, where he'd seen the gate.

Then Gou slowed down. He knew this alley, had boasted to his friends about how well he knew it now, since he'd been down it so often, searching. So he closed his eyes, coasting, no longer peddling, and lifted his nose high.

There. To his right. Jasmine beckoned. He turned his head toward it, pressing his cheek against the softer air. It was quieter there as well.

When Gou opened his eyes, he still didn't see anything but a blank wall. The hutong was there, though. The opening. Right beyond the wall.

Gou stood up on his peddles to stop his bike, then started peddling backwards, backing up his cab.

He needed speed if he was going to do this right.

And if he crashed into the wall, well, that was the will of the gods.

"Hold on!" Gou called to his passenger. He closed his eyes again and slammed down as hard as he could on his peddles. The cab leaped forward, as if it were a living animal and not made of steel and rubber.

Gou kept his nose high, seeking the start of that scent. When the air grew sweeter, and it suddenly grew quiet, he turned abruptly and opened his eyes.

The peaked gate loomed ahead of him. Gou skidded through the turn and passed through the opening with barely an inch on his right side.

"Well done," his passenger said.

Gou breathed deeply, feeling the peace settle into his bones. He was finally here. At last.

GOU WAITED IN THE TRAIN STATION, THIS TIME RIGHT outside the exit of the customs hall. He wore a better shirt now, white with a tiny red fox embroidered over the left pocket, as well as finely-made black pants, and soft leather sandals. He carried a small whiteboard with the name of his client written on it, in Japanese kanji, Chinese characters, and English.

Just like all the other official, licensed couriers.

It wasn't difficult to spot his client through the sea of travelers pouring out of the door: She was cute, with freckles scattered across the bridge of her nose, and a stillness that ebbed out of her, quieting everyone who stayed for a while in her presence. She wore her long black hair back, hiding her overly large ears, with bangs over her broad forehead. She wore a simple white-and-purple striped blouse over a straight black skirt.

"*Liequan*," she said, smiling, coming up to him.

"*Huli*," he replied. It was part of the code of the family, as well as a greeting: Hound and fox.

Gou collected her bags, carrying them easily despite their weight, like all the other official couriers did. He politely asked about her trip, but that was all, her stillness affecting him too.

Instead of leading her out to the rows of limousines and state cars, though, Gou walked her across the broad concrete courtyard in the front of the station to the rows of peddle cabs. Gou's company colors were brown and yellow, with real licenses and enough bribes that he could reserve the front parking spots.

The young woman clapped her hands with delight when she saw Gou's peddle cab. "Papa arranged for you," she said, settling into the back of Gou's cab.

"Of course," Gou replied. He'd learned a lot about his clients since that first trip on his own to *Huli Hutong*: They didn't like automobiles, and merely tolerated motorbikes when they needed speed. They preferred old-fashioned things, like handmade brooms and rickshaws.

Once all the luggage was strapped in, Gou started off at a leisurely pace, letting his client enjoy the city. Cars along the wide road raced past them, as did students on their bicycles, their bells ringing merrily. Gou took his time, though. He no longer had to hustle, racing for just one more fare.

Gou actually no longer needed to peddle a cab himself, he could have hired one more rider, but he liked to pick up family members himself: It kept his patron happy, helped smooth out any bumps in their relationship. Plus, he'd met other, stranger beings this way, building his network, hoping to become the exclusive carrier to all the spirit creatures and their kind.

Later that afternoon, Gou would take the daughter on a tour, through the tourist *hutongs*, as well as the secret, hidden ones that only the fox fairies could find.

And a few, well-trained hounds.

FUTURE/SCIENCE FICTION

I hesitate to call this section science fiction. Because while I write science fiction that's easily classified as such, the novels have more fantasy in them.

I grew up reading a lot of science fiction. I love it dearly. But I grew up primarily reading SF short stories, not novels. So I have Science Fantasy novels, none published as of 12/2018, but already written and coming.

FUTURE FICTION NOVELS

Of Myst and Folly

TO COME:
Huli Intergalactic: Origins
The Trader Trilogy
The Labors of Darius Linard
The War of the Allied Worlds

FUTURE FICTION/SCIENCE FICTION SAMPLE

THE FOLLOWING IS AN EXAMPLE OF PURE SCIENCE FICTION. It's a side story, a prequel if you will, to the Labors of Darius Linard, which is a novel written as a series of novellas.

Enjoy!

THE CARRION CROW

CAITLIN SKIMMED PAST THE DERELICT *Huang Gong* as she piloted away from the planet *Paahad.* Enough dead ships made up the space graveyard that they could form their own asteroid belt. Silent reminders of the most recent war, left to decay and fall back into the atmosphere to burn up there, a constant supply of shooting stars for the survivors to wish on.

What a waste.

The people of *Paahad* and the winners of the war—the Allied Worlds—believed that where a body fell was sacred. It couldn't be moved, but had to be interred as close to where the soul had died as possible.

Never mind that over half the dead weren't native. That they had their own families and planets and beliefs.

That entire nations mourned the loss of their sons and daughters and could never bring their bodies home, never know peace.

Caitlin steered her spaceship closer to *Huang Gong.* If the ship had been killed anywhere near one of the (formerly) independent planets, hundreds of scavengers would have been circling it, like flies massing around a dead body, reclaiming the exotic materials and metals, digging out wires and electronics.

In addition, the Family Brigade would have divers sorting through the crew cabins, searching for personal mementoes to bring back to their loved ones.

It wouldn't remain a squandered carcass, left to rot, fall apart, and burn up. To provide amusement for those on the planet below.

But the great Xinxie ship remained silent. Sterile. The bright gold of the hull tarnished with blast marks and fire, its innards gracefully spilling out into space.

The ship had been the pride of their nation. A battleship with its own fleet of fighters.

Caitlin wasn't about to get closer to the old ship, to try to dig out its remaining treasures by herself. She was alone on her ship, *Carrion Crow*, and she really wasn't equipped for salvage. Her cargo holds were already full. Plus, Caitlin herself was no longer young, able to scramble easily between blasted bits of metal.

She'd have to let her employers—the Xinxie government—know the exact position of the derelict. Maybe they could send scavengers, other smugglers like herself, to take the great ship apart.

Though they probably already knew about it. As well as who had died, and who hadn't returned.

The Xinxie were well known for their great attention to detail. The people of the independent planets had thought that when the Xinxie had joined their cause, they'd be able to defeat the Allied Worlds, or at least not be forced to join, but maintain their independence.

That dream had died as well during the battle of *Paahad*.

Caitlin sighed and nosed *Carrion Crow* up around the huge derelict, then directed her toward the edge of the *Aathgrah* system. She was ready to leave here, ready to be out in deep space again, where it was just suns and planets and huge hunks of rock to sometimes navigate around.

Not so many bones of the dead.

It had been a smooth smuggling trip so far. The space station circling *Paahad* had somehow survived the battle that had occurred over a year ago. Not intact, no, but it hadn't been reduced into rubble. Half of it had been destroyed, but it was easier to use what was there as a platform and rebuild than create a new station from scratch.

Not being fully operational made it easier for Caitlin to sneak in, her fake codes and IDs barely glanced at by the officials.

Then again, that might have been the wrinkles in her face, her age giving her the mask of propriety.

The silent crew that had loaded up the back of *Carrion Crow* had never looked her in the eye. She doubted they'd be able to identify her later.

Was it on purpose? A way of protecting themselves? Or was it shame? They were all natives, as far as she could tell. *Paahad* had been originally settled by people from the Indian subcontinent back on Earth. Like many of the planets colonized by a single group, they tended to not branch out from their original families, so had stayed short, dark haired, dark skinned, and speaking their own dialects.

Caitlin hadn't taken the time to inspect every coffin loaded into her cargo hold, but she assumed all eighty or so held the same: The remains of a Xinxie warrior, with his shield and his sword.

The Xinxie government paid well for the return of their sons.

Though if Caitlin was being cynical, the government officials cared as much about the shields as the bones. Each stood as tall as the man who carried it and projected its own self-defense and environmental system. The shields themselves were made from a rare metal rumored to be as tough as the skin of most ships.

Caitlin tapped the controls once more, setting the ship on

autopilot for the next few hours, as well as creating an alarm for herself. *Carrion Crow* wasn't big enough to generate her own hyperdrive. Out on the edge of the *Aathgrah* system waited a jumpship ready to take her (and others who'd paid dearly for the privilege and anonymity) away.

Carrion Crow was built in the shape of a squat capitol T. The bubble for the pilot's cabin, where she currently sat, was at the base of the T. Cargo holds made up the cross-beam and took up the bulk of the ship. Her own sleeping quarters and tiny workshop made up tiny bumps along the main hallway.

The jumpships—also called V ships—looked like two lines set at a perpendicular angle. Dozens of smaller ships like hers were roped into the inside of the angle, and then carried along when the bigger ship made the jump.

Caitlin unbelted herself from her pilot's chair and stood. She didn't have to sit there while the ship made its way through the system to the jumpship. The autopilot was more than capable of flying the ship on its own, without her supervision.

She grabbed onto two of the convenient handrails above her head as she floated up, then started undulating her back like a cat, stretching out all the vertebra.

She may have been old—if you called fifty old—but she prided herself on staying limber and strong.

Her pilot's chair was perfectly contoured for her, providing wonderful support for her lower back. However, after sitting in it for a few hours, even in low gravity, she still found herself jammed up.

She scratched at her shorn hair. Though she'd been continually in space for the last three years, and had shaved her long gray-streaked hair to half and inch from her scalp, she still couldn't get used to it. She cricked her neck from one side to the other, then folded herself up, stuck her feet under the rails to hold herself in place, and pushed her hands in front of her, stretching her long fingers wide.

She grimaced at the pale skin. At least she didn't have to worry about getting a sunburn when she was always inside a spaceship. She did miss the sun sometimes. Not like her fair Irish skin would have ever tanned. But maybe working outside and getting something of a tan would have hidden some of the age spots creeping across her hands.

As Caitlin stretched, she realized she'd tensed up leaving the space station. Every muscle was tight.

Why had that been? She couldn't put her finger on it. But something had seemed off. Maybe it had been the crew loading her hold, or the squat, frog-faced "official" who'd signed the false papers and given her leave to go. After he'd doubled the usual bribe, of course.

Her grandmother would have called it her *dara sealladh*, or second sight. All of Caitlin's family had it, though her mother had never believed it, calling it Old World Nonsense.

However, Caitlin had always trusted her instincts. She pulled herself back to toward the ship's console sprawled in a large half-circle around the pilot's chair and upped the range on the sensors so no one could sneak up on her.

There wasn't much else she could do, for now. She was still a few hours out from the edge of the system. She found herself yawning, then smiled to herself.

The way her face stretched told her it had been a while since she'd done that. She made herself grin, then opened her mouth widely, stretching those muscles as well.

Robbing the dead was a serious business.

Caitlin reached out and patted the crow painted across the control panels on the left side of the tiny ship cabin.

She'd commissioned the mural—about a meter and a half in diameter—when she'd christened the ship and renamed it.

The crow sat on the edge of a great battlefield. Many warriors lay fallen, dead with arrows protruding from their bodies, broken swords and shields beside them. The sun set at the far edge of the field, spreading blood red across the sky. Clouds boiled. Fog had already started gathering, obscuring some of the figures.

But there was also a star shining brightly from the sky. A single bright point of light.

Hope remained, despite the fact that Caitlin lived as a smuggler, somewhere outside the law.

She hadn't started out this way. She'd been legitimately employed most of her life. A wife. A mother.

But the war…

Caitlin still hoped that she'd find the bones of her own son Aodhan, someday. That she'd be able to take something back to her perpetually mourning family. That her husband (divorced and spending all his time living in dreams now) would survive long enough to bury his son. That her own heart might know solace.

Caitlin patted the crow one last time. The dark figure gave her comfort, actually.

Her family had called her ship morbid. But Caitlin had insisted on the new name, on the mural, on painting the outside of her ship as black as the crow.

She was finally living her life honestly. Calling a spade a spade. No longer lying to herself about her work.

It had taken her a long time to admit that all the computer programming she'd done, all the machines and equipment she'd invented, had merely prolonged the war, their original purpose twisted by both governments so they became weapons instead.

Now, Caitlin lived off the bones of the dead, like a carrion crow. She'd killed many of those who'd died, not personally, but as a byproduct of her former employment.

And as long as there was war, someplace in the galaxy, she'd have a rich life.

The alarm woke Caitlin out of a sound sleep. She'd only meant to nap for the few hours it would take to get from the planet *Paahad* to the edge of the system, but she'd been more tired than she'd realized.

She wasn't as young as she'd once been.

She blinked groggily in the darkened room. It took her a few moments to parse together what the harsh man's voice was saying: *Tracker alert.*

Damn it!

Caitlin unhooked the net-blanket that had kept her secured to her bed and then pushed herself up. She flowed up to the handrails above her head and pulled herself along, into the squat corridor and up toward the pilot's chair.

Before she sat down, Caitlin slapped the alarm button, shutting up the deep baritone.

She'd used a simulation of her father's voice for the most urgent alarms, replacing the calming woman's alto that had been used originally.

She supposed it said a lot about her that she was best served by the sound of her father yelling at her. That that voice brought all of her focus into place, and kicked up her survival instincts to the max.

Caitlin strapped herself into the pilot's chair and set her sensors to finding whoever was out there.

How had they found her ship? She'd taken an oblique route from the planet, not following any of the standard lanes that ships normally followed.

Maybe that had been her downfall. Maybe scouts tracked the off lanes.

But that didn't make any sense. There were too many paths out of the system for the Allied Worlds to track them all.

Caitlin made herself take a deep breath. Maybe it wasn't the Allied Worlds tracking her. Maybe it was another smuggler or some sort of mercenary.

She snorted at herself. As if that would be any better.

Caitlin's fingers danced across the keyboards set at the perfect angle to both the right and left of the pilot's chair. The mechanic she'd hired to create the platforms hadn't believed her when she'd told him that they were of her own design, that she'd use them both simultaneously.

Then she'd given him a demonstration.

The admiration she'd seen in his eyes had almost been enough to get her to proposition him. Except that she was too old from him.

She'd also seen that in his eyes. That the gray hair mattered.

He'd only admired her skill, not her still slim and fit body.

His loss.

Caitlin focused her attention again on the sensors.

Where was that damned ship? The one that had a lock on her?

It had better shielding than most, she had to admit. Her own sensors kept sliding off it. Plus, it was just at the edge of her range.

Finally, though, she spotted it. An anomaly. Not a presence, but an absence in space.

Behind her.

The ship was probably twice the size of *Carrion Crow*. It had six arms that spread out from a solid middle chunk. Not straight arms, like a cross, no, curved and jointed, flowing out and back in again.

Caitlin instantly recognized the design.

The ship came from the planet *Paahad* and the people there, with their gods and the many arms.

She shivered and nearly crossed herself, as her grandmother or mother would have.

Instead, Caitlin started madly adjusting her course. A *Paahad* ship meant the Allied Worlds. And they had a solid tracer lock on *Carrion Crow* as well.

Could she shake the lock?

Probably not.

But it was worth trying.

Caitlin felt the vague effect of the thrusters shoving her ship up, then down, shaking it from side to side.

They might have a solid tracker on her, and be able to follow her at a distance, but they couldn't shoot at her. Or send an electronic disrupter beam that would disable her computer systems.

Not if she was pinging around like a hyperactive two-year-old.

A cool woman's voice sounded in the cabin. "Communications requested, ma'am."

Caitlin cursed loudly, using words that would have shocked her father. If the other ship was already calling, that meant they possibly knew her. This wasn't a casual run-in between two ships passing in the night.

Albeit one that looked like a giant tick and had already rudely latched onto her.

"Yeah?" Caitlin said as she slid her finger across the comm, opening up a channel between herself and the other ship.

Might as well hear what they had to say.

"Attention, vessel RAV-346, stop immediately and prepare to be boarded," came a mechanical voice. Then it repeated itself, obviously on a loop. They'd probably assumed she wouldn't respond.

And most of the time, they'd be right.

"On whose authority?" Caitlin asked.

Don't panic. Just because they've identified your ship doesn't mean they know you and what you're carrying.

The mechanical voice cut-off mid-sentence.

Caitlin found herself straining at the silence, trying to catch sound that wasn't there.

"The authority of the Allied Worlds," came a smooth woman's voice after another moment.

She had a soft accent. The same as Caitlin's, with the vowels elongated and the consonants softened.

A familiar voice. But from where?

"Cait. Don't make me do something I'm going to regret," the voice continued.

Shit.

It was Sinéad.

Caitlin had met the woman twice. Once, when her son had been commissioned. Sinéad wasn't his direct commander—she sat further up the chain—but she'd noticed his brilliance, and had complimented Caitlin on having such a fine lad.

The second time they'd met had been when Sinéad had visited Dún Eógan, Caitlin's former home, while she'd been on holiday.

Before Sinéad had switched sides. Before she'd betrayed the independent worlds.

Before she'd ordered all of those still following her into a useless battle, getting them all killed.

"We know you're carrying contraband," Sinéad said.

"Really?" Caitlin asked. The surprise sounded fake to her ears. "What little bird told you that?"

Sinéad listed off the name of the official who'd signed the release papers, back at the *Paahad* space station. "You're smuggling eighty-eight coffins," she continued. "Xiexin warriors. You need to return them to the planet for proper re-burial."

"No," Caitlin denied. "I'm not smuggling. I'm reuniting sons with their families," Caitlin snarled.

"You are in direct violation with one of the greatest codes of the Allied Worlds," Sinéad replied. "You have disturbed the dead. Let them come back and rest where they belong."

"They belong with their people," Caitlin said hotly. "Like my son. You know how important that is. You used to believe it, too."

"I believe peace is more important," Sinéad said softly.

Caitlin snorted. "Is that what you tell yourself at night? To ease the sting of your betrayal to your own people?"

A long pause settled between them before Sinéad continued. "What I believe and why I acted as I did no longer matters. I didn't have a choice. What is important is that we've been tracking you for a long time. We know about your entire operation."

"What operation?" Caitlin asked, surprised. "It's just me. And a few families who want to properly bury their sons."

"As well as half the Xinxie government," Sinéad added dryly. "The half that's now fallen on their own swords, so to speak."

A chill went down Caitlin's spine. Though she doubted those in charge had actually been caught—politicians were notoriously slippery and always had someone else to conveniently blame—it still sounded as if there was a whole lot of trouble there. Possibly even a government coup that had happened while she'd been away.

"If, let's say, I did let you bring me in," Caitlin said slowly. "Would you tell me the exact location of where Aodhan was killed?" Even if she wasn't able to bring him home, she was certain she could get a message out.

Someone would find him and carry his bones home.

"That's classified," Sinéad said coldly.

Of course it was. The location of Sinéad's betrayal would be treated as a secret so that those involved couldn't set up crosses and create a spot for martyrs.

"That's what I thought your answer might be," Caitlin said.

She flipped up the end of her right keyboard, folding it on clever hinges.

A second keyboard lay hidden underneath, the keys registered to respond to Caitlin's biological signature alone.

"Please. Don't make me do something I'd regret," Sinéad said again. "Come in peacefully. I'll make sure that your sentencing is light."

Would the bitch actually fire on *Carrion Crow*?

Of course she would.

She'd sent her own troops to be massacred.

"Regret this, bitch," Caitlin said as she keyed in the password and new coordinates.

The alternate thrusters, the ones Caitlin had installed herself at much expense and then laughed at her own paranoia, suddenly kicked in.

Carrion Crow wasn't big enough to achieve hyperspace on her own.

But she sure could run a mean mile.

Alarms hooted and red lights flashed in the cabin. Caitlin dragged her thumb along the acceleration pad, forcing the engines to burn hotter. The smell of burnt electronics filled the air.

Caitlin couldn't outrun Sinéad. Not with that tracker lock that she couldn't shake. She knew that.

She just had to give herself a head start. Give herself some space and time to think.

If Sinéad had been following her for some time, that meant a tracker located on *Carrion Crow*.

Maybe if Caitlin found the tracker and destroyed it, she'd have a chance to escape.

Or maybe not.

Caitlin had never had the luck of the Irish that way.

Caitlin set a loud timer, counting down the minutes. She figured she had maybe twenty minutes before Sinéad caught up and blasted *Carrion Crow* out of the skies, piercing her heart with some sort of pulse or beam weapon.

Would Sinéad try to recover the bodies Caitlin carried? While the Allied Worlds gave lip service to the belief that the bodies of the dead belonged where they'd fallen, Sinéad had once believed otherwise.

Or would she just destroy *Carrion Crow* and let the bodies burn? It would be a funeral of a sort for them. The bones immolated in great fire.

Caitlin knew enough about the Xinxie culture to know that would be enough to satisfy most of the mourning families. If their dead couldn't be properly interred on their home worlds, burning the bodies would be better than having their bones lie in alien soil.

That was why Caitlin had first piloted out toward the system's edge, then raced inward, toward the sun.

If she had to make a last stand, she'd make it here, where she could burn up as well, instead of being taken in.

Anything but be captured by that traitor.

Caitlin released herself from the pilot's chair, then pulled herself along the squat corridor of *Carrion Crow*, back toward the storage holds.

It was a gamble, she knew. The tracker could be in one of two places: Either attached to the hull of *Carrion Crow*, outside and out of her reach, or it could have been placed in one of the coffins.

Since Caitlin didn't want to leave her ship, not when she had that bitch hot on her heels, she decided to check the coffins instead.

She took five precious minutes in the tiny workshop, just opposite the slip she used for her sleeping quarters, to modify a handheld scanner.

It would pick up any transmissions made from inside the ship.

The tracker probably wouldn't send out information continuously. Caitlin assumed it would ping in short bursts.

Hopefully the pattern of the bursts would be shorter than the fifteen minutes she had left.

Caitlin keyed in the code to open the storage hold. The lights stayed dim: there wasn't much to see. The room spread out on either side of the door, rectangular in shape, cold, and packed to the gills with black coffins. They were stacked one on top of another, four to a column, then roped together. Only a few of the tall columns had aisles between them.

The place smelled sterile, like dust and barren soil.

The Xinxie were as superstitious as spacers, she knew. Eight was an auspicious number, hence, eighty-eight coffins.

Four was unlucky, the number of death. Which was why the coffins were stacked that way, and no higher, though had been room for a fifth coffin at the top of each column.

Had the person who planted the tracker known it was there?

Caitlin hauled herself over to the fourth column. She ran the scanner along the long end of each coffin, but nothing pinged.

This had to be the right column, though.

Caitlin unstrapped the coffins, loosening the column, then pulled herself up to the top.

At least she didn't have to take time breaking a lock to open up the coffin.

The warrior inside had at one point been buried. Soil still clung to his matted black hair.

Barbarians hadn't even used coffins for the foreign dead. No wonder the Xiexin government was all keen on getting their sons back. They would need to be cleaned and prepared before they could be reburied.

The skin had dried to leather, though the battle had occurred merely a year before. Maybe the bodies had been treated before they'd been buried. Empty eye sockets and a gaping jaw looked back up at her, twisted, as though he'd died screaming.

Thankfully, she didn't see any blood, and the smell of rot was faint. She suspected that given time, and a warm room, that would change.

White satin covered the inside of the coffin, pure and unblemished. Who'd paid for such an extravagance? All Caitlin wanted was a plain wooden box to hold her remains when she went back to the earth.

"Sorry," Caitlin said as she quickly patted down the inside of the cover first, then felt along the edges of the box, trying not to touch the body or disturb the great shield. The satin felt smooth under her fingers, warming quickly.

Nothing.

Caitlin wished she could slam the cover back down but there wasn't enough gravity for such an action: It would have sent her flying up toward the ceiling.

Instead, she closed the cover down gently, then, after bracing herself, shoved the coffin to the side so she could get at the next one. The first coffin floated mournfully in the air, as if waiting to be taken to the next plane.

Her handheld pinged when she reached the third coffin.

There.

Caitlin opened the coffin cover.

A red light blinked at her from inside the white satin, in the coffin lid, directly over the warrior's face. The light went out quickly, as if ashamed of having been discovered.

"Sorry," Caitlin said to the warrior inside. He was in much worse shape than the others had been. She took a knife from her belt, then cut out the tracker from the inside of the coffin lid with one hand while she used the tip of a fingernail of the other hand to keep the head of the body from floating up and away.

With a sigh of relief she pushed the lid closed and examined her prize.

It glowed once more in her hand, red and malevolent, a great seeking eye like something from an old-fashioned children's book.

Caitlin couldn't tell the manufacturer from just looking at the piece. She'd have to take it apart.

And if she had the time, she might have. Teased apart the circuits and the signal, maybe gotten it to broadcast a false location.

As it was, her countdown was already nearing its end. Less than five minutes remained before the other ship neared.

Instead, Caitlin went to the side airlock, at the far end of the cargo hold. In addition to the larger hatch for goods, she'd installed a second, smaller one, for sending probes. It was more efficient to open up a smaller door rather than the larger one.

Caitlin spaced the tracker with relish, pushing the button to space the bugger with as much emphasis as she could.

Now, it was time to see how well this old bird could still fly.

———

CAITLIN SHOOK HER HEAD. THE PILOT'S CABIN SMELLED LIKE sweat and burnt plastic, never a good combination.

The view from her pilot's chair wasn't pretty either. The sun loomed large on her right side, blotting out all the stars.

There wasn't anywhere else for her to go. She'd tried everything she knew, retuning her own jamming signal, racing from one end of the system to the other, heading out of system, then heading back in, but she just couldn't shake Sinéad.

Then her father's voice came on again. "You're too hot!" he yelled at her. "Systems are about to overload."

Cursing, Caitlin flicked the warning voice away.

It wouldn't last. She'd programmed it to come back on in five minutes, knowing her own impetuous nature.

And maybe that was why Sinéad had been able to follow Caitlin so well. Somewhere, in her traitorous heart, there still burned the desire to be free.

The woman's alto came on next, startling Caitlin. "Communications requested."

Really? *Now* the bitch wanted to talk?

"Fine," Caitlin snarled. She opened up the communications channel.

"This is a recording," same Sinéad's voice through the cabin. "I will not fire on an unarmed ship. But you leave me no choice. I've asked for help."

"Message received," Caitlin said, subdued. What the heck had Sinéad done? What kind of "help" had she asked for?

A buzzing noise filled the little cabin. For a moment, Caitlin was reminded of spring on the coast of her home, when the bees came out of hibernation and swarmed all the beautiful flowers.

Then she realized what exactly Sinéad had done.

Who she'd sent.

Drones.

Not just any drones. The special seeking ones that Caitlin had inadvertently created.

She'd patterned their behavior on the dolphin-like creatures that men had brought with them to the stars, modified and released into new worlds' seas.

The dolphins, as well as Caitlin's probes, learned from each other. Helped each other. Communicated and directed each other without external guidance.

She'd originally created them to help find and recover lost spacemen and equipment.

The government had been the ones that had taught them to hound a victim.

And to kill.

This was so very, *very*, not good.

Sinéad's ship turned and raced away, out of the local area, out of the heat, leaving the drones to do their dirty work. Caitlin's sensors picked up a circular object where Sinéad's ship had been. Probably one of the larger probes with the engine removed so it was no longer maneuverable.

A platform from which to broadcast Sinéad's signal.

Caitlin turned *Carrion Crow* toward the platform.

The mass of drones filled a quarter of screen like a black cloud.

They weren't paying attention to her.

Yet.

They focused on the small probe that Sinéad had left behind, the platform still broadcasting her last message.

Even from that distance, Caitlin saw the sparks as the probe was disintegrated.

She swallowed around a hard block in her throat.

The mass of drones didn't have a head or a tail.

But she still knew when they'd turned away from the current task, toward the next one.

Toward her.

Caitlin flung *Carrion Crow* back around, flying toward the sun, knowing that she'd never make it. The drones would catch her and haul her back before she could immolate herself.

However, she was determined to take as many of the drones with her as she could.

———

CAITLIN SCANNED FURIOUSLY AS SHE FLEW, TRYING TO LEARN as much about this pod of drones as she could.

They were a much newer model. Several generations beyond her first iteration. Each drone was about the same size as a human, more than a meter long. They were all shaped similarly to *Carrion Crow*, like a capitol T, except that the arms were not perpendicular to the center piece, but curved down slightly, toward the body.

Maybe she'd liken them to a crossbow.

One of the advantages to the flatter design was that they could stack up, one on top of another, easily adding themselves together to haul a larger mass.

It also meant they could form a solid wall, interlocking arms and lining up head to tail. There weren't enough of them to block her. However, they could create a large enough mass to distract her from the other group that had come sneaking up from behind.

Fortunately, she'd recognized the pattern and changed her own course, from a straight line to an unpredictable path, so they couldn't capture her.

The original drones that Caitlin had created had to always had a pod leader. The leaders were a touch more sophisticated than the others. But the pod would still function even if the leader malfunctioned.

It took her a while to find the leader. Seemed the same sort of shielding that Sinéad's ship had used had been applied to the drone leader.

It wasn't the same shape or size as the others in the pod. Instead of being long and flat, cruising through space like an arrow, it was ball shaped. Maybe two and a half meters in diameter.

Caitlin realized that the pod leader could carry a human. It would be cramped and uncomfortable, and wasn't intended to be used for long-term space flight. Standing room only, no place to lay down. No food supplies or workspace.

But from the pod leader, a human could then interact with the pod, could teach it new tricks.

If the person in the pod leader was smart enough, he or she could also learn from the pod.

It gave Caitlin an idea.

She continued her mad rush toward the sun. *Carrion Crow*'s shields were already at their max, already too warm. She set up an auto pilot, continuing her insane course.

Now, to make the dead pay for their passage.

She patted the crow painted on her wall one last time before she hauled herself away from the pilot's cabin.

If she'd been as superstitious as some of the other spacers she knew, she might have kissed two fingers of her right hand and touched the star as well.

Hope lived.

She just wasn't sure if it was actually within her reach.

CAITLIN OVERRODE THE LIGHTS IN THE STORAGE HOLD, bringing them up to full.

She'd never appreciated before what an ugly space it was. All gray and hard. It still smelled like dust. The lights reflected dully off the black coffins, as if they couldn't abide any brightness.

Caitlin paused, then crossed herself like her grandmother or mother would have.

Truly, time to live up to her name of *Carrion Crow*.

The four coffins that Caitlin had loosened earlier had all ended up toward the top of the storage hold.

She wasn't about to go chase them down. Instead, she undid the straps holding the closest coffins, bracing herself and shoving them apart. She opened the first one, dragging out the Xinxie warrior's shield, then shutting the cover again before the bones could escape, apologizing to its former owner.

The smell of rot seeped into the air. One edge of the shield felt sticky.

Caitlin didn't look closely enough to determine if it was dried blood.

The shield itself was a work of art. Ancient Chinese characters swirled across the front of it, black on a rich red background. A solid silver border outlined the shield, at least a hands-width wide. Where the border had been nicked, Caitlin saw circuits.

The underside of the shield revealed a control panel. Holes lined the middle of the shield—maybe that was where the shield would have locked onto the bearer's arm. A dull blackish silver metal made up the shield.

Caitlin had never believed the rumors of how tough the shields were.

And either the rumors were true, or she'd join the warriors soon.

As quickly as she could, Caitlin freed three more shields, apologizing to the owners each time.

She told herself that her work didn't have to be pretty. It wouldn't be judges on its aesthetic.

It just had to work.

She bound the four shields together, making herself a rough box.

Caitlin checked her supply belt, making sure she had everything she could gather there: credit sticks in other people's names, a couple of blue energy spheres worth triple their weight in credits, saved just for this type of emergency, stim tablets that would keep her awake and drive away her need for food.

Then she crossed herself one last time, attached the helmet to her EVA suit, slid into her box made of shields, and pressed the detonator, blowing open the cargo hold doors.

The drones would investigate the ship, she knew. Unless her luck was spectacularly bad, the drones would assume that her ship was merely coming apart. She'd hidden the bomb well.

The sudden change in air pressure sucked Caitlin and the rest of the coffins out of the hold, into space.

Carrion Crow shuddered, then sped away, its route already set.

She anticipated that at least half, if not more, of the drones would follow after it.

Divide and conquer.

The heat from the sun, so close, burned Caitlin, oppressive and malevolent. She screamed as the shields pressed in around her, their circuits flaring and sparking.

But the unexpected lightshow had the desired effect.

One of the drones, as curious as the porpoises it had been patterned after, came to see what the this new thing was.

Caitlin had once been a fisherman's daughter. She knew how to cast a wide net.

Her arms were confined by the coffin-box of shields protecting her. Her net was less than a meter wide. And she was casting without gravity.

She still snagged the drone on the first try, drawing it closer.

Though the drone's shape had changed, its bones were the same as the ones she'd created.

There, in the armpit on the right side, was a physical switch that sent the drone flying back to the leader.

Fortunately, these drones were stronger than her original breed.

The captured drone obediently flew away.

Dragging Caitlin along behind it, like so much flotsam.

It didn't take Caitlin much to override the controls of the pod leader, opening the hatch and letting herself in.

It was as small as she'd figured it would be. Cramped. Full of electronics and waldo arms that could be used to repair as well as program the other members of the pod.

Caitlin didn't have much time. She had to get the pod leader offline. Make it seem as though it had flown too close to the sun.

Then figure out how to pilot it away. Get herself to a jumpship. Make her getaway.

As Caitlin worked, she thought about Sinéad. The other woman had claimed not to have a choice in regards to her betrayal of her people.

Maybe that had been the case.

It wasn't as if Caitlin or any of her people would ever forgive Sinéad the traitor.

But maybe, maybe, Sinéad had given Caitlin a chance. One that she'd never had.

Given Caitlin the chance to get away.

Sinéad knew that Caitlin had created the drones.

Perhaps Sinéad had guessed that if anyone could figure out how to escape from the drones, to turn them to her own purpose, it would be Caitlin.

Caitlin knew that this was another chance for her. The opportunity to walk away. She was dead, now. She could never use her existing name.

She could disappear. Create a new life for herself. Find work away from the old battlefields.

Caitlin snorted at herself.

As if.

Caitlin wasn't about to walk away from her new career.

Someone had to reunite the living with their honored dead. Maybe if she could have found the bones of her own son, given her family the peace they needed…

No.

A carrion crow couldn't change the color of her feathers.

She'd remain in the dark shadows until every warrior was reunited with those who remained behind and mourned.

IMMERSIVE FICTION

WHILE I LOVE WORLD BUILDING AND COMING UP WITH NEW magic systems and new characters, Franklin and his kin are in a world of their own. It's a quiet place. Franklin is deliberate. Determined. If the world's about to end he's still going to stop and open the door for his lady first, not just run away screaming.

IMMERSIVE FICTION NOVELS

The Chronicles of Franklin:

The Popcorn Thief
The Soul Thief
The Child Thief

IMMERSIVE FICTION SAMPLE

The Franklin Chronicles are set in rural Kentucky. They would count as contemporary fiction. But the pace is slower. The world, richer. The tastes and smells deeper.

Take a breather. Come walk with Franklin for a while.

This is the first chapter from Book One of The Franklin Chronicles: "Franklin Versus The Popcorn Thief".

FRANKLIN VERSUS THE POPCORN THIEF: CHAPTER ONE

FRANKLIN'S ALARM RANG TOO DAMN EARLY, AS IT did every morning. Still, he didn't dawdle, or indulge himself by hitting the snooze button. Instead, he got out of his narrow bed, pulled the tan sheets up to make it neat, then walked through the dim bedroom to his tiny bathroom for a shower and his weekly shave, scraping carefully against his dark skin for the few errant hairs.

Putting on his brown Kroger uniform, Franklin hummed to himself, pleased that his weekly workouts with the Ab-Buster were keeping him in shape, just like the man on the TV had promised. He didn't pull the shades of his bedroom windows up until he was ready to leave the sanctuary of his room: He never knew what kind of ghosts might be waiting for him out there.

This morning, though, his view of his field of popping corn was unobstructed by any ghostly visitors. He spent some time looking at the front stalks. He only had five long rows, twenty stalks per row, and each one was precious to him. Winds had been light the night before, and he didn't see any damage. Broad green leaves grew out evenly from the tall stalks, and nestled in between them were the fluffy tassels of the best popping corn in all of Kentucky.

Yellow corn, of course. Franklin didn't go in for fancy strawberry corn, or that black kernel stuff. He grew grade A, American popping corn, using a hybrid seed that he'd paid good money for so it would mostly pop up into butterfly flakes, that were longer and more tender than the mushroom-shaped flakes.

And this year, he was gonna beat Karl Metzger, his old high school rival. Franklin's corn would finally win the blue-ribbon prize for the best popping corn at the Kentucky State Fair. He'd be able to hang that ribbon right there, above his dresser, between the pictures of his long dead papa and his recently dead mama. Make them both proud.

Satisfied, Franklin finally opened the door to his bedroom. He didn't know why the ghosts couldn't cross the threshold—maybe because no one but him had ever been in there, not since Mama had died, and she hadn't been in there that often. Still, he kept the door closed, as he didn't want to see their faces staring at him in the dark.

Sunlight beamed against the living room windows. The couch and overstuffed armchair lurked as dark shapes against the wall. It was gonna be a hot one today. Franklin left the shades down to give the house an edge against the heat. He turned on the ancient TV sitting on the even more ancient bureau to listen to the farm report as he made his way into the kitchen.

"Morning, Mama," Franklin said to the ghost sitting at his kitchen table.

Mama didn't say anything, as usual. She looked the same, her hair all done up nice, her good gold hoops hanging from her ears, wearing her best Sunday church dress. Being a ghost had faded out her black skin, brought out freckles across her nose that Franklin had never seen.

But it hadn't dimmed the glare that she frequently gave

Franklin, like she did that morning.

Franklin tried not to take it to heart. He reasoned that being a ghost was hard on a body, particularly someone like his mama, who'd worked at the local beauty salon in town just so she'd have people to talk with all day. Not being able to say a word or touch anything—not even push a piece of paper across the table—had to be difficult.

"Corn's looking good this morning," Franklin told her as he got the peanut butter out of the top cupboard and the bread out of the breadbox sitting in the corner of the green linoleum counter. "I'll go out and check the fields when I get home. There's some weeds that need pulling." He got an egg out of the fridge, and reached for his lard.

He paused.

The cover of the mason jar wasn't tightly screwed on. It just rested there, with the lid seal off kilter.

"Mama, did you do this?" Franklin asked as he pulled the jar out.

She didn't reply.

"God—dang it!" Franklin said, unwilling to swear in front of Mama, even though she was a ghost.

Franklin had only opened that jar of lard last week; now, it was mostly empty.

Mama still glared at him.

This was Franklin's special lard, rendered down, white and pure from Sweet Bess, the pig he'd slaughtered earlier that spring. Sweet Bess had been anything but sweet. She'd been barely tame, rummaging in the woods next door for her food and only coming to the pen when the cold winter rains started. She was also a killer. Any chicken or small animal stupid enough to challenge her got eaten by her. This made her meat extremely sweet, smelling almost like perfume when Franklin cooked up her bacon.

Ghosts loved anything salty, would lick it up like a cat with cream. And though good lard would never go bad sitting out, Franklin kept it tightly sealed in the fridge.

So how the heck did a ghost get to it? He'd never met one who had the strength to open a jar. No ghost had ever haunted the refrigerator before, either.

"Mama, who was the greedy ghost?" Franklin asked, looking directly at her, hoping she'd give him some clue. "'Cause they ain't here now." All of the ghosts who haunted Franklin tended to stick around until he'd done his duty and helped them pass on, leave this earth and move to wherever it was that they was supposed to be.

Mama had never showed any intention of doing anything but sitting at Franklin's kitchen table for the rest of her death. She'd been sitting there for almost a year now.

But Mama didn't say anything, just glared at him like she did when he made a mistake that was, according to her, "too stupid for words."

So Franklin went back to fixing his breakfast—a fried-egg-and-peanut-butter sandwich. He screwed the lid on tight on the tiny bit of lard left and put the jar back in the fridge, hoping there'd be enough for his popcorn later that night. It wasn't corn he'd grown, he'd already run through that, and this crop had at least another couple of weeks before it'd be ripe. The first time he'd put Sweet Bess' lard on popping corn he'd nearly licked the bowl clean, but Mama had been staring disapprovingly at him from across the table.

He still didn't understand how a ghost had opened that jar. Or how it'd gotten into the fridge.

The weather report from the TV confirmed that it would be a hot one. Franklin finished his breakfast, washed his dishes, brushed his teeth, then got ready to go.

"I'll be home usual time, Mama," Franklin called out as he left the house. Then he stopped and checked over his shoulder just in case, but no one was passing by the driveway, which was open to the quiet street.

Not that it would have mattered—everyone in town already thought Franklin was crazy. Some of them even knew he sometimes talked with ghosts: Mama had bragged on him at the shop more than once. She'd always told him that it was important for him to do his duty to the poor folks who were stuck between worlds, even when it sometimes meant trespassing or asking strange questions.

From the front shed, Franklin got out his bike. He checked the chain, thinking that maybe that strong ghost had gone after anything greasy. It looked fine, though. No ghosts had messed with it.

Though Franklin could drive, cars were expensive, plus, he didn't like to take chances like that. If a ghost suddenly popped up while he was riding his bike, he could just fall over. In a car, he might hurt someone else.

Franklin didn't have to share the lane with any cars. He waved at Mrs. Wilkerson, out watering her geraniums, before he turned onto the bigger street. Here, he rode along the gravel edge, hearing his mama's voice, warning him how dangerous Stevens Road was. Cars whizzed by, nearly blowing him over.

But there was nothing for it. Franklin pedaled the two miles as fast as he could, huffing up the small hills, then coasting down the other side of the rolling street. The chorus of cicadas blasted him on either side. Fields of tall sorghum blocked his view of anything else, followed by neat rows of tobacco. The sky above him paled in the heat, with high clouds to the west.

From Stevens Street, Franklin turned onto the shoulder of the four-lane highway. Just as it narrowed down to two lanes, he passed by Metzger's Farm stand, with people already waiting in line.

Franklin pedaled by furiously. Everything that Karl Metzger turned his hand to grew bigger and better tasting than whatever Franklin tried. But Franklin was still going to beat him this year, get that blue ribbon prize for himself. His corn was growing well, and he had plenty of time to experiment with drying it, removing the perfect amount of moisture so each kernel would pop up tender with great wings.

The highway became Jacobson Avenue, and Franklin steered over to the sidewalk. Though he liked the shade of the trees, they also broke up the sidewalk, making it dangerous to ride along. Franklin tried to concentrate on it, and not spill over (again), but his thoughts kept going back to the ghost and the lard.

What was he dealing with? It must be a mighty strong ghost. Why hadn't it stuck around, to let Franklin know what it needed in order to pass on and stop haunting him?

As Franklin pedaled hard up Main Street, he shivered once, like something had just walked over his grave.

That ghost was something different.

And different was never good.

***

FRANKLIN DIDN'T MIND THE TOMATO STAINS DOWN THE FRONT of his brown Kroger uniform, or the dirt on his knees from kneeling to stock cans of sweet corn on the lower shelves. However, he'd also had to uncrate a box of that awful men's body wash, and of course, one of the bottles hadn't been sealed right. He could barely stand himself as he biked home as fast as he could, bumping over the broken sidewalks then along the four-lane highway, trying to create a breeze to blow the stink off him.

He didn't know if ghosts could smell or not. He figured they couldn't, though, so he wasn't worried what Mama would think.

If she'd been alive, she might have accused him of rolling in a back alley with some cat in heat, despite Franklin never having a girlfriend. He couldn't imagine bringing home any girl that Mama wouldn't rip to shreds.

Franklin rushed into the kitchen, intending on going straight to the shower. "Mama, I—"

He stopped when he saw Mama had company.

Or rather, he had another ghost, sitting at the kitchen table with Mama.

None of his other visitors had ever dared. What made her special?

She'd been as black as Franklin when she'd been alive. He wondered if she'd worked with Mama at the beauty parlor 'cause she had bleached blond hair that curled softly around her face, the obvious result of hours of work and product. Her once-bright red lips framed perfect teeth, and the color on her long nails matched her mouth. She didn't look much older than Franklin either, which was a shame—he hated it when people passed on early.

She also had some power, as she clicked those nails impatiently on the table, the only sound in the whole house.

Click. Click. Click.

Was this his greedy ghost from the night before?

Most of the time, Franklin only got impressions of what a ghost wanted, their *intent*. He rarely got a name, but hers came through, shining like her hair.

Gloria.

"Miss Gloria, it's nice to meet you," Franklin said. He would have been polite to her whether Mama had been sitting there or not —she'd raised him to do the right thing.

He didn't expect a reply, and he didn't get one.

"Is there something I can do for you?"

Nothing came, no hint of a place Gloria wanted to go to, or something she needed doing before she passed.

That surprised Franklin: Since her name had come through so loud, he'd figured her purpose would come as well. "Well, ladies, if you'll excuse me, I have to freshen up before dinner."

Both Mama and Gloria glared at him, as if this was too obvious.

Maybe ghosts did have a sense of smell.

If it had been just Mama, Franklin would have taken off his

shirt in the kitchen and thrown it down the stairs to the basement right then. But that wasn't right, undressing like that in front of a strange female ghost like Gloria. So Franklin went back to his room to change.

Nothing was different there: The bed still had the sheets pulled up, his photo of Papa (who'd died when Franklin was two) and one of him and Mama still hung on the wall above his dresser, an empty space between them, where his blue ribbon would go. Franklin threw the offensive shirt into the laundry basket, then gathered up the rest of his dirty clothes. It was only Monday, and he generally did laundry on Tuesday, but this shirt couldn't wait.

He looked out at his field. He'd go pull weeds after he put a load in the washer.

Mama and Gloria hadn't moved from the kitchen table. They almost looked like mother and daughter, except that Mama would have called Gloria's shirt indecent. The top button was undone and it strained across her chest. If Gloria had worked for Mama, Mama would have made her go home and change.

Franklin started the washer, with extra vinegar for taking the smell out of the shirt, then eagerly went outside.

The air still held the afternoon heat, but the shade from the trees out back promised the coolness of the evening. The taller stalks of corn reached their heads up high to catch the last of the sun's rays. Scents of warm earth and growing things floated up to Franklin. The slightest wind set the corn to rustling.

Franklin looked out from his field to the land next door. It was sitting fallow, the For Sale sign weathered. The State Fair prize wasn't enough money to buy it, but maybe, with that money, he could talk Mr. Averson into lowering the price. Franklin had a bit saved, left over from Mama's insurance money—most of which he'd used to pay off the house, so he only owed taxes on it every year.

But wishes weren't fishes, like what Mama would say.

Franklin knelt down between the rows and pulled up one some

ragweed. He wouldn't ever spray—he'd heard too many horror stories of farmers ruining their food crop with the wrong weed killer. He made a note to get the long-handled dandelion digger later when he spotted a couple of those ragged leaves.

Franklin stood after a bit, wiping his brow with his kerchief. Weeding wasn't hard work, but it was constant. He took that as a good sign—everything was growing so well in his tiny field this year. He was sure to win that prize, finally.

A chill went down Franklin's back, not caused by any wind. When he turned, he jumped and took a step back. He hadn't expected Gloria to be standing so close.

"How can I help you?" Franklin asked. It was always best to be polite, especially with ghosts out in the corn field. They always gained strength there. Franklin had stopped going out into his field at night years before: Too many ghosts followed him there, trying to push their *intent* on him, enough so that he felt his skin turn sticky.

Gloria just glared at the stalks, as if somehow they'd done her wrong.

"Were you married to a farmer?" Franklin guessed.

Gloria shook her head. Sadness flowed out from her, like water from a broken hose.

Finally, they were getting somewhere. It was always a good sign when a ghost started reacting to Franklin: It meant they were looking for his help; that they might be thinking about passing on.

Mama had yet to react to anything Franklin said. He was afraid she intended to haunt him until *he* died.

"But you loved a farm—a farmer?" Franklin asked.

Gloria gave a hesitant nod.

Franklin sighed. This was gonna get messy. Ghosts with love on their mind were the hardest to satisfy. He hated this part of his duty to the ghosts, trying to figure out what a person that couldn't really talk wanted, who often wouldn't even respond when he did ask a question.

"Did he love you back?" Franklin held himself ready to bolt, but Gloria didn't do more than glare at him.

"So he loved you," Franklin said, relieved.

But Gloria didn't agree to that either. Instead, she shook her head at his corn and faded out of sight.

What did that mean? Had the farmer loved her? Or not?

And why did they have to come bother him about it?

Franklin sighed and returned to his crop, to the easier cycle of growing and watering and trimming just right, so much better than the complicated dance of the living and the dead.

THE NEXT MORNING, GLORIA DIDN'T RETURN UNTIL FRANKLIN was getting his bike out of the front shed. Clouds filled the sky, and the sticky air made Franklin feel as though he hadn't dried off after his shower. It would storm that afternoon. At least his crop was well enough established that unless it hailed, the stalks could withstand a strong wind.

"Good morning, Miss Gloria," Franklin said softly after making sure that no one walked on the empty lane out in front of the property. "Can I give you a lift into town?"

He'd done that before. Seemed like a ghost could ride on the basket, between the handlebars. Only two weeks before, he'd given a ride to a little girl (too young) with pigtails and a simple dress, who'd wanted a lift to the county judicial center just up the street from the Kroger so she could go harass the drunk who'd mowed her down.

Gloria took one look at his bike then raised one immaculately plucked eyebrow.

The *Are you kidding me?* came through loud and clear.

With a quick shiver, Gloria disappeared.

Franklin groaned. She was going to haunt him all day at the Kroger, he just knew it.

Was she strong enough to pull down a shelf? She was stronger than most ghosts, able to click her fingernails against the kitchen table. Franklin wasn't looking forward to finding out.

FRANKLIN COASTED HIS BIKE WEARILY DOWN MAIN STREET. The good news was that Gloria hadn't been strong enough to knock things off shelves. She was, however, a bad influence on kids. Somehow, just being near her was enough to make the younger ones cry and the older ones pick fights. Twice today, Franklin had had to stop teenagers from throwing cabbages or potatoes or whatever was handy at each other.

The storm promised by the dark clouds and heated air hadn't come. Wetness pressed down on Franklin as he cut across to Jacobson. He'd need another shower when he got home, though it wouldn't matter. He felt like he was riding through one already.

To lift his spirits, Franklin rode across Jacobson and up Stewart, turning north, heading toward what he called the sculpture garden. The Sorrels were from Los Angeles, come to his small town of Katherinesville to retire. Adrianna called herself an artist, while her husband, Ray, indulged her. She filled their yard with "found art": fallen tree branches wired together into tall, eerie men; pieces of glass collected from the highway and pasted together into stars; even plastic bags tied together and dyed, turned into colorful streamers.

Once a year, the Sorrels had a huge picnic. They invited all their neighbors and at least half the town to come and eat at their place. Tables ran the length of the yard, filled with fresh rolls, heaps of sliced ham, potato salad and coleslaw and corn on the cob and green beans and everything else neighbors brought to share, with ice cream at the end.

Gossip was that the Sorrels were some kind of Hollywood behind-the-scenes royalty. But they acted like regular folk—well, mostly—and if the gate door was open, Franklin would stop and chat for a while.

But the gate was firmly shut that afternoon. They did have a new piece hanging on the wooden fence, a strange metal cabinet with tiny plastic dolls pasted around the edges, framing it.

Was that really art? Franklin had no idea. He found beauty in his fields, in fresh growing things, in neat stacks of apples or well packed rows of carrots at the store.

And in the clean lines of kernels, after they'd been dried, ready to be popped.

Franklin headed north for a few more blocks. The houses were a mixture of old and new. Some of the buildings were colonial, made out of brick and tall, with many chimneys and clean, steep tin roofs. Some were more modern: rectangular and one story, from the '50s, like Franklin's. Green Kentucky bluegrass covered the yards. Despite the dry summer, purple flowering pawpaw trees bloomed overhead, brightening the day.

Just as Franklin had seen enough and was turning back toward Jacobsen, Gloria appeared, not two feet in front of him.

Though Franklin knew he couldn't hurt her, he still automatically swerved onto the grass edging the side of the street. His tires skidded, and Franklin fell.

"Dang it!" Franklin said as he stood up, brushing off his Kroger uniform. A green and black smear went down one pants leg. He was gonna have to do laundry twice this week if this kept up.

When Franklin looked up, Gloria stood unmoving like a sign post, one hand pointing away from Jacobson, up the street, farther into the neighborhood.

With a sigh, Franklin got back on his bike and pedaled the

direction Gloria indicated. She appeared again, pointing him this way and that. Where was she wanting him to get to? How long was this going to take? His stomach rumbled. Not too long, hopefully.

Finally, Gloria stopped at the end of a dead-end street, in front of two ramshackle houses, and pointed to a trail going up between them.

Franklin shook his head as he got off his bike. It was bad enough that ghosts haunted his place. He hated it when they made him trespass.

But at least the houses looked dark, the owners not home. Trash lay piled up on the front porch of the one, with blue sheets of plastic covering the windows. Broken toys lay in front of the other.

Hopefully, neither of them had a dog in their backyard.

Franklin looked up and down the street. He didn't see anyone else there, waiting or watching. Damn it. He took a deep breath, squared his shoulders, and walked his bike up the trail Gloria was pointing to.

The backyards of the two houses were cleaner than the fronts. This was where the folks here lived, with lots of benches, chairs, and tables for them to gather at. They shared a long barrel smoker, and the smell of their recent BBQ made Franklin's mouth water.

Past the yards was a fallow field, full of brambles and sharp leaved weeds. Franklin pushed his way through, not bothering to untangle vines from the wire wheels of his bike. Hopefully no one minded his trespassing. Maybe, though, this would be the last of Gloria's haunting.

Finally, Gloria pointed Franklin toward a field.

Was this her farmer's field? Maybe he really could help her pass this afternoon.

Plus, corn grew in this field. Franklin happily walked into it. The stalks were tall, well groomed, and healthy. He judged the crop to be a little behind his rows: Maybe the farmer hadn't watered as much as Franklin had.

Gloria joined Franklin, marching angrily down the stalks toward a taller plant. Was there a particular place in the field that she cared about? Had something happened here?

Then Gloria stopped, holding out her hands in front of her.

Even from a few feet away, Franklin felt the wave of power that Gloria pushed out of her palms. She grew darker, less ghostly, as she pressed her will against a single ear of corn. But it wasn't hate that drove her, no.

It was fear.

What made her so scared of that corn?

Finally, Gloria got her prize, and a single ear dropped off the stalk and onto the ground. Gloria glared at Franklin, pointed at him, then down at the ear of corn.

Despite the heat, Franklin got a cold chill up his spine. He checked over his shoulder, but he didn't see another ghost. He scanned carefully, closely, but all he saw was more stalks of corn.

However, something else lurked there; a silent watcher. He just knew they weren't alone. Maybe some spirit haunted these fields.

With great reluctance, Franklin walked forward and picked up the ear of corn.

As soon as Franklin touched it, he knew Gloria's *intent*: She wanted him to steal this corn, steal all of this farmer's crop.

What had that farmer done to her, that she wanted Franklin to ruin his livelihood? It must have been real bad. If she'd been alive, she would have been shaking with fear. Something about this corn and this field scared her worse than any ghosts could have.

"I'm sorry," Franklin said, as gently as he could. "I can't do it. I can't steal this corn for you. You're gonna have to find something else to help you pass on." He'd never help a ghost to that extent. Not even if the person they was mad at had done something horrible. Gloria was just gonna have to find another way.

Gloria tipped her head back, turning her eyes up to the sky, then opening her mouth and screaming. Her face held sheer agony, like all the pinchers of hell was grabbing at her.

Franklin had never seen such a display.

Then Gloria marched over to Franklin and *pushed* at him, trying to get him to do her will, to leave all the stalks bare, dry, and leafless, like gravestone markers in the field.

"I can't," Franklin said, backing away, his skin feeling like it was being wrapped in sticky cobwebs. Gloria was strong, but no ghost was strong enough to force the living to their will.

Gloria stopped, paused, and gave a sly smile.

Suddenly, Franklin knew who owned this field: Karl Metzger, his rival for the Kentucky State Fair blue ribbon prize for growing the best popping corn. The man who had everything Franklin wanted. His old rival.

Franklin dropped the ear of corn he'd been holding, like it was suddenly hot enough to pop all on its own. He raced with his bike along the long row and bolted out of the field, onto the highway, then pedaled like mad back toward town.

How could Gloria think he'd be so…so…dastardly as that? It just wasn't right.

Franklin would never do something like that, particularly not to a rival. He wanted to win that prize, wanted that blue ribbon so badly—but he'd do it on his own terms. He'd never stoop to cheating that way.

As Franklin got to his side of town, turning off the four-lane highway onto Stevens, the clouds opened up and blinded him with rain.

It didn't matter to Franklin that he had to walk his bike the rest of the way home due to the downpour, that Mama glared at him all through dinner, that he had to use the last of Sweet Bess' lard melted over his popcorn that night: he was content, 'cause he knew he'd done the right thing.

He also knew this was far from over.

HISTORIC/EPIC FANTASY

I started off writing historic fantasy with "Paper Mage". I wrote two other historic fantasy novels ("The Caves of Buda" and "The Jaguar and the Wolf"). However, I stopped writing for a while after that. When I returned, my tastes had changed. I wanted to write other things.

This new world of publishing has enabled me to do just that—to explore all the worlds that I encounter.

However, I do keep returning to my first love.

HISTORIC/EPIC FANTASY NOVELS

Historic Fantasy

Paper Mage

The Caves of Buda

The Jaguar and the Wolf

A Sword's Poem

Epic Fantasy

When the Moon Over Kualina Mountain Comes

The Glass Magician

The Desert Heart

The Ghost Dog

HISTORIC/EPIC FANTASY SAMPLE

YOU'LL NOTE THAT THERE ARE SMALLER ISLANDS NEARBY THE historic fantasy island. These are epic fantasy pieces. They're set in the past—perhaps not *our* past, but a recognizable past. I keep writing there too.

The following is a short story that works as the prequel to the novel, "The Glass Magician."

Enjoy!

THE BLOOD HOUND

The blood hound following Myrizhah flopped down in the street outside the tinker's shop Myrizhah entered. She knew better than to think the hound would grow bored and leave while she shopped. Even if she tried going out the back, or ran away on the fastest horse, it would still find her. No woman escaped the blood hounds.

Still, Myrizhah couldn't help but stop and glance through the tinker's shop window back at the hound, who lay there in the dusty dirt road like a regular dog. He was medium sized, coming up to about her knee, with short, red-brown hair and tall, pointy ears that stuck on the top of his head. His nose was black and took up a disproportional amount of his snout. His eyes were just a shade lighter than his fur. The hound looked sad and too aware, as if he had seen too many babies die.

No one bothered the hound. Most avoided him, either crossing the street or walking a wide path around him.

Despite his ordinary looks, people could *feel* that he was something special.

Myrizhah turned away, looking back into the shop. It was only lit by the window overlooking the street, making it seem dark and crowded. Hanging from the walls were small brass pans for cooking eggs, large iron kettles for stew, tiny pewter cups given to newborns, and even finely decorated tin squares that could be hung on a wall, merely for decoration.

It was a rich person's shop, despite how tiny and dimly lit it was. It smelled of clean coins, fancy brass polish, and iron shavings.

Myrizhah wasn't rich. But she wanted to give her unborn son the best.

"I see a hound's got your scent," said the tinker, coming out from behind his counter to stand beside Myrizhah. He was an older man with many fine wrinkles around his blue eyes. He wore his white hair to his shoulders while his face was clean shaven, as was the custom here. He had a bulbous nose and flabby lips, with heavy jowls.

It was the type of face Myrizhah had gotten used to here, up north, as opposed to the knife-thin and sharp features of the men she'd grown up with in the south, with their darker skins and full beards.

"Congratulations," the tinker continued.

Myrizhah nodded and reflexively put her hand on her extended belly, as if to protect it. Blood hounds only followed pregnant women whose babies had magic.

It was considered an honor up here, in the north, to birth a baby of power. Something else that was very different from where Myrizhah had grown up.

"Ducca the midwife has declared the baby will be a boy," Myrizhah told the tinker.

"I see," the tinker said, nodding. "You want something to bind him here."

"Yes," Myrizhah said. "A horseshoe made from an ore dug in the nearby mountains."

It was custom both in the north as well as the south to place a horseshoe, the symbol of the Goddess Onnet, on the belly of a woman as she was giving birth, to help draw the baby out. In ancient times, the first letter of Onnet's name had always been carved as the symbol Ω.

A magician's magic was tied to the land, usually close to where he was born. While a magician might have some small power over all the trees, he could do amazing things within his small, local forest. A magician might have an affinity for rock, but he could only perform great magic with the granite mined in a specific range. Same with water workers, who worked best with their personal creek or lake.

This babe had to be tied here so Myrizhah could leave him behind with a clear conscience when she escaped the family she'd been married into and ran away back to the south.

The tinker cast a sly glace at Myrizhah's clothes, obviously calculating her wealth. Then his eyes rested on her belly for a moment and grew softer.

"I'd recommend a horseshoe made from the tin found near the Agrafa pass," he said kindly. Then he grew shrewd again. "Unless you'd prefer something from the silver mine…"

"Tin would do quite nicely," Myrizhah assured him.

Her mother-in-law didn't deserve a grandson who worked with silver or gold, though magicians who worked with metal were rare.

Not that her mother-in-law would have thought such fortune possible. Not from her bad luck daughter-in-law, the one who had already caused the family such grief.

The son she carried kicked suddenly, as if to distract her dark thoughts. Myrizhah couldn't help her gasp. That boy took her breath away, sometimes.

Too bad she would never see him grow up.

"May I offer you a chair, madam?" the tinker said, taking her arm.

Myrizhah stopped herself from pulling away and shouting at the man. No one in the south would ever presume to casually touch her that way.

Instead, she let herself be guided to a guest's chair that was just before the counter. Though the pillow was covered in fine, red linen, it was stuffed with straw, hard and practical.

She refused the tea the tinker offered her, though she did take a cup of cool water.

The boy kicked again. The pain he offered her was almost rhythmic, though she didn't think these were contractions. Not yet. As this was her first child, she had to rely on Ducca the midwife, who told her the babe wasn't due for weeks.

Still, she put down the cool cup and started bargaining with the tinker. Though she might be short of breath, she wasn't addled, and she could still strike a good deal.

When Myrizhah left the shop, her tin horseshoe in hand, she paused for just a moment. It was bright out here, the air in the mountains cooler and drier than what she'd grown up with. The dust in the air smelled the same though, and despite their strange clothes and manners, underneath, the people here were the same too: poor and just trying to get by.

The hound had already risen, giving her that too-knowing look.

It didn't care what her plans were after the baby was born. All it cared about was the babe.

There were stories of hounds who'd "helped" during difficult births, killing the mother but saving the child.

He wouldn't get her, though. This baby would be born with ease.

Then Myrizhah was going to run away. Leave the harshness of the mountains, the softness of the trees, the rich black dirt.

Go live in the desert again.

Even if she died trying.

DUCCA THE MIDWIFE WAITED FOR MYRIZHAH AT THE TINY farmstead. It wasn't much bigger than a shack—just a single room with a shelf for her bed and a hearth at the back—but at least it gave Myrizhah a place to live away from the family compound where the rest of her in-laws resided.

Myrizhah knew better than to look around, to hope that her husband had returned from the war. He'd gone off just after they'd discovered she'd become pregnant, with a cheery promise that he'd return in a month, having made his fortune as promised by the *Padisha-i-Ghazi*, the great emperor.

News of his death had made her mother in law, as well as the rest of the family, turn cold to his foreign wife.

Myrizhah understood. They thought she was bad luck.

The fact that she was carrying a son, as well as a magician, had warmed their reception of her only slightly. They were still regularly awful to her, and she wept many hidden tears.

Ducca took one look at Myrizhah then took her by the arm, bringing her closer to the fire.

Myrizhah couldn't help but stiffen. Did everyone have to touch her today?

Ducca was a tiny woman, barely coming up to Myrizhah's ample breasts. Myrizhah always felt like one of the giantesses from the tales standing next to her. However, Myrizhah could also feel the strength in Ducca's hands, how firmly she held Myrizhah. This was no weak, pampered woman.

Ducca wore her blonde hair braided. It shone like gold in the firelight. Just like her husband's had. It had been one of the reasons why Myrizhah had agreed to marry him, to travel so far north, away from her family and everything she knew.

She still hoped his son would have that fine, golden hair.

"This babe is as impatient as you are," Ducca chided. "He's

dropped." She reached for Myrizhah's belly, then paused before she touched her. "May I?" she asked.

Myrizhah nodded. Though it wasn't proper for a stranger to touch a woman, this was a midwife. And she did need to know the condition of her charge.

Ducca's strong fingers probed Myrizhah's belly.

Myrizhah kept her mouth closed firmly as she felt the nausea rise.

"The head's down," Ducca told her. "He's coming. Tomorrow or the next day."

Myrizhah nodded, relieved and anxious at the same time. She hadn't finished her preparation. She did have a bundle of travel clothes already prepared. When she'd leave would depend on how quickly she'd recover her strength. If she didn't have to hold the babe, she knew it would be easier to leave him, but she'd never seen a woman just walk away from a birth.

"Have you named him yet?" Ducca asked.

Myrizhah shrugged. She'd told her in-laws early on that it was her people's custom to not speak the name of an unborn out loud, not until after they were born. It was too easy for a curse to be put on the unborn.

It was an old wives' tale. However, Myrizhah didn't believe in curses, not like that. She'd never given the baby a name because she'd never wanted to be that close to the boy.

She was only going to bear him. Then she was going to leave.

Ducca crossed her arms over her chest and scowled. She wore short sleeves that showed off her muscular arms, along with what they called "trous," full pants that looked like a long skirt. She shook her head. "You'll change your mind when the babe is born," she said softly.

Myrizhah raised herself up to her full height. "What are you talking about?" she asked disdainfully.

"You'll come to love the boy," Ducca told her.

Mryizhah merely blinked at the midwife, unsure how to reply. She wasn't going to be there long enough to love him. Then she shrugged. "I'm told that happens," she said.

Ducca nodded. "I have promised to go to Farmer Tiegan's house, to check on his wife. I only promised because I had thought your son was weeks away, not days." She scowled at Myrizhah's belly, as if the boy was purposefully vexing her.

"Go," Myrizhah told her. "I'll be fine."

"I could stop at the main house, get your mother-in-law or one of your sister-in-laws to sit with you," Ducca offered.

"No," Myrizhah said immediately. "Not until the birth is closer," she added when she saw Ducca's shocked look at her strong refusal.

"All right," Ducca said. "I won't be long. I promise."

Myrizhah knew the woman prided herself on her keeping her word. She was always directly honest with everyone. Myrizhah found it off putting at times, refreshing at others.

Ducca had no children of her own. Which may have been why she was so concerned with others having healthy births.

"I have the hound here to help as well," Myrizhah said with dark humor.

Ducca glanced over toward the door of the tiny farmstead. The hound was waiting on the threshold as always, in his usual guard spot.

Before the baby was born, he would protect Myrizhah. That was true of all the blood hounds.

After the baby had started coming was an entirely different matter.

"I'll be back so you won't need his help," Ducca said earnestly. She threw a cloak over her shoulders and hurried out the door.

The room seemed colder without her presence. Myrizhah carefully picked up another piece of wood and threw it on fire. Pregnant women were supposed to be warm all the time, but

Myrizhah was cold up here in the north, where the sun was so pale.

Soon, she would be warm again, back in her own southern home. Her family wouldn't necessarily welcome her back with grand feasts of pomegranates and fruit wine—she should stay with her husband's family, even if she found them intolerable. But she hoped she'd be less unwelcome there.

Myrizhah thought she'd spin a little more by the firelight but found her eyes drooping. Instead, she laid down on the tiny shelf and napped, instantly dreaming of holding the tiny tin horseshoe like a dowsing rod in her hands as she marched across endless sands, but the tin had no affinity for the land and it couldn't lead her to water, no matter how far she roamed.

———

PAIN.

Myrizhah dreamed of an iron poker shoved into her belly, the pain of it making her cry out.

When she opened her bleary eyes, the pain didn't recede. It took her a moment to place the dark wooden roof above her head, not the canvas of tents or the stucco of the towns.

She was in the north, where it was always cold, with a family who hated her and would just as soon she died in childbirth.

Not that her mother-in-law had said such a thing directly to Myrizhah. However, the woman had refused to pray for her and only said prayers for the unborn son.

He was the only thing of value to them, and only if he turned out to be powerful.

They would all soon find out.

The child was on its way.

Myrizhah had no idea what time it was. Had she been asleep for hours? Or a fraction of that time?

Another rolling wave of pain washed over her. Powerful contractions emanated from her nether regions and up her belly.

Yes, this boy was as impatient as his father had been the first time they'd lain together as man and wife, taking her roughly, then drying her tears and doing it the right way, as a real man should, with tenderness.

There was nothing tender about birth, though.

Ducca had taught Myrizhah a rhyming song to help her to breathe through the contractions.

Myrizhah hadn't bothered to tell the midwife that unlike her northern sisters, she knew how to count far past the fingers on her hand. Still, she tried to hum the song as she slowed down her breathing, getting ready for the first awful push.

Something cold touched Myrizhah's hand, bringing her back from the world of pain. Turning her head took a monumental effort, but she still managed to peer out beyond the edge of the bed.

The hound stood there, dark and glowering.

"Oh no," Myrizhah said. "You don't get to help. I can manage this on my own."

Then another contraction hit and the room grew dark.

Myrizhah knew there was something wrong. She'd seen childbirth before, had held her eldest sister's hand to help ease her through it.

There was too much pain. The blankets beneath her were soaked with too much blood.

Myrizhah hadn't done any stitching for the last four weeks. Nothing should be blocking the birth canal.

But that was how it felt. As if the baby couldn't get out.

Myrizhah cried out as the next wave hit her. She had to do something, anything. Or she might take a knife to her own belly to end this.

Wait. Where was the horseshoe? She'd gone to sleep holding it.

The metal felt cool to Myrizhah's sweating palm. She raised up her tunic and slid the horseshoe onto her belly.

The pain doubled, the horseshoe sticking to her skin as she writhed.

What had the tinker given her? Had he poisoned the metal? She couldn't pull it off—it stuck to her skin as if glued there.

Myrizhah wailed in grief. She had to live. Had to see the desert again. Had to get this baby born.

Coolness touched her fingers again.

With horror, Myrizhah looked to the side.

The hound was there, looming. He had grown bigger than the medium-sized dog he had always appeared to be, and now would come up to her waist, easily. His coat had changed as well, growing black as a curse.

"No!" Myrizhah screamed as the hound grew taller. He placed one paw—now larger than her own hand—on the side of the bed shelf. He lowered his muzzle to her belly, his hot breath easing her pain for the moment.

Myrizhah braced herself for the next part—when the hound tore her belly to bits, killing her in order to save the boy.

Instead, the hound licked her belly, licked at the tin horseshoe, drawing it up in his mouth, much more delicately than Myrizhah would have expected.

Suddenly, Myrizhah could breathe again. The pain instantly lessened.

What had the tinker given her?

A whining noise made Myrizhah look to her right, to where the hound stood.

He had turned the horseshoe, holding the curve so the tin ends stuck out from his mouth like odd-shaped fangs. Then, the hound shook his head. He moved so quickly his head became a blur.

A soft *pop* filled the room when the hound stopped, as though a cork on a barrel of beer had just been loosened.

The horseshoe was no longer tin.

The hound raised himself back up, carefully placing one paw on the bed shelf, then putting the horseshoe back on Myrizhah's belly. It felt cool against her skin and the pain receded another fraction.

Myrizhah craned her neck to see the horseshoe, running her fingers along its smooth surface.

It was now made of clear glass shot through with ribbons of gold and green.

The colors of the old kings. Before the *Padisha-i-Ghazi*, the magician emperor, had come to power centuries before.

Then another wave of pain struck Myrizhah. It was a normal pain, though. Something she'd seen other women bear as part of childbirth.

With a determined cry, Myrizhah pushed, as impatient as the babe to have the birth finished.

The head crowned with her next push. It was too late for Myrizhah to stagger over to the birthing chair so she could at least catch the baby with her arms. Instead, she gave another great push, the shoulders sliding out followed by the rest of him.

It took all the stubbornness Myrizhah had to make herself sit up, to reach for her babe, to awkwardly draw it up across her sore stomach.

The hound licked at the boy's foot, causing him to jerk and cry, drawing in his first breath, letting loose with a healthy wail.

"Shhh, shh," Myrizhah said, cradling the boy's head.

She didn't care for the boy. She couldn't. But she could hold him and comfort him, just this once.

A shadow crossed her sight.

The hound had levered himself up to the side of the bed again, looking down on her.

He seemed to be asking her permission.

Myrizhah collected the boy's feet up higher on her body and gave the hound a sharp nod.

One giant paw reached out and pressed on her belly, hard.

Myrizhah couldn't help but shout with pain once again as her body had yet another contraction. The afterbirth came sputtering out.

The hound moved from the side of the bed to the foot, where he greedily devoured the afterbirth. Then he looked up at her, licking his bloodied chops.

Padisha-i-Ghazi thanks you for your contribution.

Then the hound disappeared, a great wind chasing him.

Myrizhah shivered. She was going to have to clean up this mess, soon. Clip the umbilical cord. Say the prayers to Onnet, thanking her for the live birth, the healthy son.

Then she realized what the hound had said.

He would go directly to the emperor and vomit up the afterbirth. Then the emperor would take a piece of the afterbirth and fashion it into a scale, that would be sewn into the great cloak he always wore.

No magician could attack the emperor in his cloak. They couldn't harm their own blood.

This was why the blood hounds had been conjured. To protect the emperor.

For the hound to speak to her meant that her boy was a magician of great power. That the emperor himself would one day fear.

Then Myrizhah looked down at the boy.

He had both hands clenched tightly around the glass horseshoe, resting his cheek against it.

With a sinking feeling, Myrizhah realized that she was going to have to take the boy with her when she left.

Metal, stone, iron—these were the materials the northern magicians had an affinity for.

Glass—basically sand blasted with such heat that it melted—was a material that only a southern magician could use.

He could only come to power in her lands.

She would have to name him now.

Maybe Alpheais, after his father. Or Trulliç, after hers.

She could decide later.

For now, she could sleep, rest a little, content that she would be going home.

ABOUT THE AUTHOR

Leah Cutter writes page-turning fiction in exotic locations, such as a magical New Orleans, the ancient Orient, Hungary, the Oregon coast, rural Kentucky, Seattle, Minneapolis, and many others.

She writes literary, fantasy, mystery, science fiction, and horror fiction. Her short fiction has been published in magazines like *Alfred Hitchcock's Mystery Magazine* and *Talebones*, anthologies like Fiction River, and on the web. Her long fiction has been published both by New York publishers as well as small presses.

Find Leah's books here.

Follow her blog at www.LeahCutter.com.

Reviews

It's true. Reviews help me sell more books. If you've enjoyed this story, please consider leaving a review of it on your favorite site.

Come someplace new...

Are you a traveler? Do you enjoy exploring strange new worlds, new cultures, new people?

Journey into the various lands envisioned by Leah Cutter.

Sign up for my newsletter and I'll start you on your travels with a free copy of my book, *The Island Sampler*.

I will never spam you or use your email for nefarious purposes. You can also unsubscribe at any time.

http://www.LeahCutter.com/newsletter/